I'm not a BEAR

Soft cover edition first published 1985 by
Buttercup Books Pty Ltd, Melbourne, Australia

First published in U.S.A. 1987 by
The Australian Book Source
1309 Redwood Lane
Davis, California, U.S.A.

© Text, Denise Burt 1984
© Photographs, Ron Ryan 1984

ISBN 0 944176 00 3

Typeset by Graphicset, Mitcham, Victoria
Printed and bound in Hong Kong by Colorcraft Ltd

I'm not a BEAR

DENISE BURT
photography by
RON RYAN

THE AUSTRALIAN BOOK SOURCE

I'm not a bear!

A lot of people think that koalas are bears,
but we are not.
We are marsupials.

Koala mothers like this one have a warm pouch in which her baby lives for the first six to eight months of its life. Then the baby rides on its mother's back for a few more months.

This one is nearly a year old, so he'll soon be looking after himself.

Koalas are related to the wombat. Wombats are marsupials too. They are ground animals and eat roots and grass.

Koalas live in the tops of eucalypt trees and eat the tender leaves.

The good leaves are often a long way up. There's not much to eat on this branch.

After all that climbing and eating we sometimes fall asleep right where we are . . .

or settle down to a good scratch.

Crossing the road in wildlife reserves can sometimes be dangerous.

Some drivers forget to watch out for us. We are a "protected species".

Koalas are better at climbing trees than crossing roads.
Our sharp claws make it easy to go straight up . . .

and hold on when we get where we want to be.

Our claws also make it easy to hold on and eat at the same time.

And they are wonderful for those itchy spots.

We don't need much water.
There is all we need in the nice juicy eucalypt leaves like these.
In the early morning they have cool dew drops on them too.

We don't need many teeth either, though a good strong tongue helps.

There's nothing to eat here.
Jumping into the next tree is quicker than going down and up again.

Some of us aren't so good at jumping yet. It's a long way to fall.

Life is usually peaceful until there are too many koalas in one place.
Then the Wildlife Rangers have to move some of us to another area.

We don't like being moved so we snarl and grunt. But they don't hurt us. They take us in sacks to a place where there's more food. And we like that!

There always seems to be a lot of visitors.
Koalas are very popular.

But sometimes the people come too close.

We often pretend we're asleep and hope the visitors will go away.

But the little ones are curious and won't sit still.

It's sometimes hard to find a warm quiet spot for a sleep.

Ah . . . that's perfect.

Look who's here!
It wasn't such a quiet spot after all . . .

And it's windy too!

Koalas are

sometimes itchy,

sometimes sleepy,

sometimes busy,

sometimes grumpy,

but we are **never** bears.

KOALAS
Phascolarctos cinereus

The word 'koala' comes from an Aboriginal dialect and means 'no water'. The Aborigines observed that the koala did not need water as other animals did.

The koala is born blind and hairless when it is not much bigger than a bean, at about five weeks. It wriggles through the mother's fur to her pouch. The mother helps this grub-like creature by licking her fur to provide a 'path' to her pouch.

Once inside the pouch, the baby attaches itself to one of the two milk teats. It stays in the pouch for about six months, where it develops thick fur, powerful legs and claws. As it grows bigger and stronger, it pops its head out of the narrow vertical opening to the pouch.

When the baby is strong enough to leave the pouch, it climbs on to its mother's back. Even with a baby in this position, the mother can move easily from tree to tree. The baby's strong claws grip the mother's thick fur firmly and ensure a safe ride.

The koala's front paws have the thumb and first 'finger' close together, with the other three making up a second section. The toes on the hind legs are separated and both front and hind paws have soft padded soles, making them ideal for climbing and holding.

Koalas are found in coastal areas throughout north eastern and southern Australia. The northern koalas are slightly smaller than those in the south and their fur is shorter and not as thick to enable them to cope with the hotter climate in the north.

Although passive by nature, koalas will defend themselves if cornered. They assume a squatting position and make boxing motions with their forearms, slashing wildly. Their razor-sharp claws could rip a man's skin to the bone.

The koala is protected by law, but it was not always so. In the early days it was hunted and killed for its thick fur. In the early 1920's, over 2 million pelts were sent out of the country. In addition to the unlimited killing for their fur, the koala numbers were reduced by bushfires, disease and land clearing. The koala came very close to being wiped out completely. Fortunately it was realised in time that their numbers were down to a few thousand and steps were taken to halt the decline.

Hundreds of surviving koalas were relocated in areas where suitable trees were plentiful and their numbers began to increase. The law now deals very harshly with anyone who kills or injures a koala or who keeps one in captivity without permission. But even with this protection, large numbers die each summer in bushfires. Man has also passed on some of his own diseases — like the common cold — against which the koala has no immunity.

Constant care and protection are necessary to preserve this appealing little Australian marsupial which, like the kangaroo, has become a national symbol.